# TIME FOR BED

Mem Fox

# TIME FOR BED

ILLUSTRATED BY

Jane Dyer

HARCOURT, INC.

Orlando   Austin   New York   San Diego   London

www.HarcourtBooks.com

Library of Congress Cataloging-in-Publication Data
Fox, Mem, 1946–
Time for bed/Mem Fox; illustrated by Jane Dyer.—1st ed.
p.  cm.
Summary: As darkness falls parents
get their children ready for sleep.
ISBN 978-0-15-288183-2
[1. Bedtime—Fiction.   2. Animals—Fiction.   3. Stories in rhyme.]
I. Dyer, Jane, ill.    II. Title.
PZ8.3.F8245Ti      1993
[E]—dc20      92-19771

X  Z  BB  DD  EE  CC  AA  Y

The paintings in this book were done in Winsor & Newton
watercolors on Waterford 140-lb. hot-press paper.
The display type and text type were set in Goudy Old Style.
Color separations by Bright Arts, Ltd., Singapore
Printed and bound by Tien Wah Press, Singapore
Production supervision by Warren Wallerstein and David Hough
Designed by Camilla Filancia

For Allyn and Louise,
because this book needs two more stars
—M. F.

And for Barry,
because this book needs a bear
—J. D.

It's time for bed, little mouse, little mouse,
Darkness is falling all over the house.

It's time for bed, little goose, little goose,
The stars are out and on the loose.

It's time for bed, little cat, little cat,
So snuggle in tight, that's right, like that.

It's time for bed, little calf, little calf,
What happened today that made you laugh?

It's time for bed, little foal, little foal,
I'll whisper a secret, but don't tell a soul.

It's time for bed, little fish, little fish,
So hold your breath and make a wish.

It's time for bed, little sheep, little sheep,
The whole wide world is going to sleep.

It's time to sleep, little bird, little bird,
So close your eyes, not another word.

It's time to sleep, little bee, little bee,
Yes, I love you and you love me.

It's time to sleep, little snake, little snake,
Good gracious me, you're still awake!

It's time to sleep, little pup, little pup,
If you don't sleep soon the sun will be up!

It's time to sleep, little deer, little deer,
The very last kiss is almost here.

The stars on high are shining bright—
Sweet dreams, my darling, sleep well . . .

good night!